# Henry Hobbs, Space Voyager

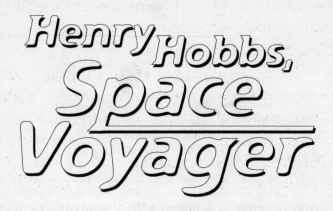

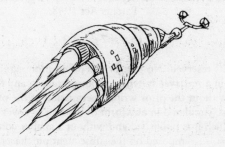

Written by Kathryn Cave

Illustrated by Chris Riddell

Hodder
Children's
Books

a division of

D1342431

Text copyright © 1990 Kathryn Cave
Illustrations copyright © 2001 Chris Riddell

First published in Great Britain in 1990
by Viking under the title *Henry Hobbs, Alien*
This edition published in 2001
by Hodder Children's Books

10 9 8 7 6 5 4 3 2 1

A Catalogue record for this book is available from the
British Library

ISBN 0 340 80579 X

Printed and bound in Great Britain by
Guernsey Press Limited, Guernsey, Channel Islands

Hodder Children's Books
A Division of Hodder Headline Limited
338 Euston Road, London NW1 3BH

# Contents

# 1 – First Day Back at the Omicron

It is always the same.

At the start of term the teacher comes in. He thumps on his desk but nobody hears, they are all thumping too. So then he shouts, "All right, quiet down in the back row. Stop that at once, Gonzo, if you break that desk you will have to pay for it out of your lunch money. Sit down and be quiet all of you. I have to take the register."

He takes the register. "Arthur? Henry? Gonzo? Take him to the medical room, boys, it is his own fault, desks were not meant for doing headstands. Charlie? Reginald? Do not fuss, boy, it will stop bleeding in an hour or two. And don't drip on to your maths book, you have a rough book, don't you? What are you doing down there, Matthew? Anyone would think it was your nose that was bleeding. No, you can't go to the medical room too, it is full up. Put your head between your knees till you feel better." And so on until at last he is finished.

Then he gets down to business.

"All right, class," he says, "for homework this weekend I want you to write about what you did in the holidays. At least four pages, proper ones, not cut in half like some boys did last term. Good handwriting too, and if you do not know how to spell a word, look it up. Don't use 'got', it is sloppy and boring, and don't use slang either, you are ten years old now, you should know better. Watch out for punctuation, I want lots of it, and don't forget the paragraphs, I am fed up with page after page without a break, it gives me a headache. Hand it in on Monday morning first thing and stop fooling about, Henry. I have been watching you, and you too, Arthur. It has been an exciting week but it is over now, the whole planet is in quarantine for fifty years, it will not be exciting again in a hurry. If I hear one more word about squodgy green humanoids and stuff that sounds like the prehistoric comics our ancestors brought here from Earth hundreds of years ago, there will be trouble. All right, class, get out your books. Yes, it is geography, Henry, it is always geography first thing on Monday. Since you are so full of energy, you can hand out the new books."

That is Mr Thomas, my teacher, but he is no worse than the others. And one thing you can be sure of: although they say they want to hear what you did in the holidays, they do not mean it. They couldn't care less what you did provided you write it neatly and get the spellings right. It is grammar all the time with them. The truth comes nowhere. This is a fact and everybody knows it.

So why am I going to all this bother, writing pages and pages, not just four, for someone who will not appreciate it and will send it back, probably with something written on the bottom like, "A good try, Henry, but not what I asked for and you must do something about your writing"? It is not easy saying what happened to me in the holidays. There is a lot of remembering to do, not to mention looking words up in the dictionary. Why go to all the trouble when I could hand in what I wrote last year and Mr Thomas would never know the difference?

The answer is that I have been talking to someone I know, and he says, if I don't write what really happened, no one will.

He won't because he is trying to forget most of it.

Lieutenant Jones won't because he is still on the pills and they won't let him have a pen or any sharp instrument.

Major Razumov can't, which is a good thing because although it was an accident, I never liked him.

It has to be me who writes the truth then. I owe it to history.

What follows is the absolutely true story of what I did in the holidays. It is a good story, and the best bit of all is that I am here to tell it. I very nearly wasn't.

## 2 – Omicron and Rolo

There are four hundred and twenty-nine planets in the known universe. (Don't ask me how they are so sure because I don't know and neither does Mr Thomas. "Good grief, boy, look it up in an encyclopaedia if you are so interested," he said when I asked him this morning. But I wasn't that interested and so I still don't know.)

Anyway, you can forget about four hundred and twenty-eight of those planets, including the interesting ones like Mega and Philippon, because this story is not about them. It is about Omicron, which my geography book says is the smallest and least significant planet known to man. That is the only time it mentions Omicron in the whole book. We are not even on the map at the front that has the other planets on it.

"Why doesn't it say anything here about us?" I asked Mr Thomas. "About what it's like here, and things like that?"

"We know what it's like here, Henry," said Mr Thomas. "That is bad enough, especially now term has started, we do not want to read about it too. Ah, there goes the bell at last. Put your books away, class. No, not like that, Gonzo, use your head. Good grief, I did not mean head it, boy, have you gone mad? Stand back, Arthur, and let me have a look. Well, that is not too bad, nothing some Sellotape will not fix. Put Gonzo over there where he will not get in the way. Off you go, enjoy your break. I certainly intend to."

This is all very well for those of us who live on Omicron. But what about all the others who will one day read this story? We are not in their books, they do not see us on their television, I bet we are not in their newspapers either. If they pick up this book they will say, "Omicron? Never heard of it", and think "What rubbish", just like Mr Thomas but for different reasons.

Well, this is not fair, but there is not much I can do about it. I can't write the history of Omicron by Monday, and if I did, would you read it? I don't think so. I will put in useful bits every now and then, when I remember. You'd better not skip them, though: I don't want to put them in for nothing.

Now you are almost ready to get started. You have met me, and my friend Arthur (whose dad is the landing-station manager), and Mr Thomas. You can't meet most of the others yet because when the story starts I do not know them. I know Rolo, though, worse luck. He was there right at the beginning of the story too, so I can't put off describing him any longer.

Here he is: Rolo, my brother, on the morning it all began.

Rolo is fifteen years old. He is big, like the picture of a gorilla in our biology book, but not so friendly. He has muscles everywhere, because he does press-ups every night before he goes to bed – a hundred, usually. I can tell by counting the times the building wobbles.

On the morning it all begins I am sitting

on my own in the kitchen. Mum has left for work at the food plant. Dad left years ago so he is not there either. Rolo is still in bed.

Suddenly the Earth shakes, there is a noise like thunder. This is Rolo getting up. THUMP THUMP THUMP he comes pounding along the hall towards the kitchen. CRASH the door flies off its hinges. Rolo has arrived. His face is furrowed, fire flashes from his nostrils. He is always like this at breakfast.

Today he has a jar crushed in his enormous fingers. He pushes it underneath my nose. "Have you been using my hair cream on your models again? Have you?"

"I hardly used any."

"Why's it all gone, then? Look." I can see the jar's empty, he's practically pushing my nose into it.

"It's not my fault." Trust Rolo to blame me for everything.

"If you touch any of my stuff once more, just once, you're going to wind up like a plate of porridge. You had better believe it, Henry. This time I am not JOKING." His voice goes up and he thumps the table with his massive fist. WHAM WHAM! The Earth rocks, the windows rattle. It's a miracle the building is still standing.

The cereal packet has fallen over, spilling purple cornflakes all over the table. I scrape up a bowlful and pour on a carton of long-life vegetable substitute. There's no point talking to Rolo when he's in this sort of mood. He won't see reason.

He pounds the table a few more times, then scrapes himself a helping of cornflakes. I pass him the sugar. He growls and aims a blow at my right ear as he takes it. He is calming down.

I wish I had a brother I could talk to, so I could explain about the hair cream. It's not as if I *want* to use it, I would say to him. That cheap grease does terrible things to model buggy engines. I'd rather use lubricating oil any day, but what am I supposed to do when I run out of it? Just tell me what I am supposed to use but hair cream, I would like to say to Rolo. And yes, I have tried toothpaste, but it doesn't work.

I could say this to Rolo, but I would be wasting my breath, he wouldn't listen. When I have finished the cornflakes I take a look at him. He is chewing with his eyes shut. He looks almost human.

"Why don't you buy some decent hair gel next time, Rolo?" I say as I get up from the table. "If the cream does that to my engines, imagine what it's doing to you. I'm joking, Rolo, I'm joking."

He has got no sense of humour, Rolo. I have to move at the speed of light in order to leave the apartment alive.

Underneath the apartments is a garage for space cruisers, bicycles, broken furniture and that sort of thing. I pop in to look for a cricket stump to use as a laser gun because I have arranged to have a space battle with Arthur later that morning.

Somebody has broken the stumps, but Rolo's pump is clipped on to his space buggy so I take that instead. There is no point going back to ask permission, he never lends anything. If he wants the pump and can't find it, it will be his own fault: I would have asked him if he wasn't so selfish.

I tuck the pump under my anorak and head for the landing-station.

## 3 – The Landing-station

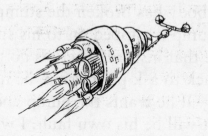

The landing-station is on the edge of the settlement – a long walk or a short sprint, depending on whether or not Rolo is after me.

At the perimeter fence I slow down to a trot and duck through the hole in the netting, by the sign that says:

No one uses the main gates. They are so rusty, if you opened them they would fall apart. Arthur's dad doesn't like anyone to touch them.

Inside the fence it is lovely. There is long grass and flowers and butterflies. You can find all sorts of stuff too. Last year Arthur and I found a tailfin from a Mark-3 Space Cruiser. We took it to the settlement museum and the man there said it must be over a hundred years old. It is in a special case in the museum now – you can go and see it if you want to.

The long grass goes right up to the landing-strip but then, of course, it is all different. Arthur's dad says you can't let the grass grow everywhere, not on a landing-station. The north end of the strip is carrots this year, the south is cabbages, the emergency landing-area is runner beans and the marrows are round the patch of concrete where the shuttle docks on Tuesdays. (The only navigational equipment the shuttle has is Dave, the pilot. He says the marrows help him to see where to land.)

The manager's office is a wooden hut next to the emergency landing-area.
A sign outside says:

It is the oldest building in the settlement. Arthur's dad offered it to the museum once but they didn't have a case big enough.

You have to be careful visiting the office in summer because the vultures who nest in the satellite dish don't like strangers, even me, and they see me every day almost. Today it's all right though. The sun is slanting down through the clouds and the vultures are sunning themselves on the office roof. I duck my head and run for it. I am through the door and into the office before they even open their eyes.

Arthur is in the office already, waiting. We are going to play Earth Invaders on the station computer before we have the laser battle.

"OK if I switch on, Dad?" Arthur asks.

His dad is lying on the sofa with his eyes shut. "Mmmm," he says, so Arthur switches on. Arthur and I are the only ones who use the station computer. Arthur's dad doesn't play himself, he says the screen give him a headache and he can never remember which button to press. As soon as Arthur and I are through, he will switch off. He

18

says, why waste electricity?

"What if someone wanted to send us a message?" I asked him once.

He rumpled my hair and laughed. "Life's not like that, Henry," he said. "Nobody sends messages to Omicron."

"Not ever?"

"Maybe when the station was first built. But not since then."

"Why not?" I asked.

"Why should they?" said Arthur's dad. "Are you expecting a message, Henry? Friends on Earth, maybe? An invitation to Philippon? I tell you what, I'll leave the system on tonight so they can get through, I promise." Then he went and lay down on the sofa again. I like Arthur's dad, he is very good at joking.

That morning starts with the normal argument over who has first go at Earth Invaders. In the end Arthur says, "Well, it's my dad's computer." He sits down and sets up the game.

Arthur's dad is stretched out with his feet on the desk and his head on the printer. "Do you mind if I use your anorak, Henry?" he asks after a few minutes. "This equipment is so badly designed it is impossible to get comfortable on it. Thank you, Henry."

He folds the anorak and puts it between his head and the printer. "In a modern station I would not have to do this," he says, wriggling his neck to get settled. "In modern stations the printers are quilted." He shuts his eyes and for a while there is no sound but the whine of rocket blasters and the scratch and thud of vultures on the roof.

Then it happens: the printer starts to chatter.

"Cut it out, Arthur," says his dad. "I have a hard day's weeding ahead."

"Don't blame me," says Arthur, not looking round. WHAM WHINE KAPOW go the Earth Invaders. "I'm not doing anything. It must be Henry."

"Me? I don't even know how it works." All the time the printer is chattering RAT-TAT-TAT. "It must be doing it by itself," I say to Arthur's dad, who has sat up, frowning.

He takes the anorak off the printer. At once a sheet of paper shoots out and the chattering stops. "Look," I cry, "it must be a message!"

"Less noise back there," says Arthur, still busy at the keyboard. "This could be an Omicron record." (Every time he scores over 100 he says that.)

Arthur's dad has picked the sheet of paper up and is studying it. He looks stunned, and no wonder. The last message to reach Omicron was the one cancelling the space cruiser service indefinitely – that was when Arthur's great-grandfather was landing-

21

station manager. Another reason Arthur's dad looks stunned is what the message says, which is roughly this:

```
(577888{{£@66668?'"]+++—) (8&&%444£21
£2) (— — [p?=%%4$$2@!
/&*%%)££@"??) (****@?????????
```

"Is it in code?" I ask. Arthur's dad turns the paper over and looks at the back without speaking. The back is blank. He turns the paper upside down and holds it up to the light. "Can you understand it?" Still no answer. "Why don't you ask them to re-transmit?"

"Ask who? If you can show me which bit is the address, Henry, I will be grateful."

"You could look up the transmission manual."

Arthur's dad says that long ago his grandfather used a book to block up a hole in the gerbil run. It was a very big book, but they were very big gerbils. They ate it and escaped. He thinks that book was the transmission manual.

He paces to and fro, looking worried.

"Somewhere in this galaxy someone is sitting behind a big desk in a proper office full of comfortable sofas and quilted printers, waiting for an answer from Omicron.
What is he going to do when he doesn't get one?"

"Sit down, Dad," says Arthur, "you're in my light."

"For crying out loud, Arthur, this is no time for Earth Invaders. My career is at stake. Look!"

There is a terrific WHINE CRASH BANG. The game is over. "That would have been a record," Arthur says, "for certain." He looks at the piece of paper his dad is waving under his nose. "The printer's set wrong, Dad. You must have put your head on a button."

Arthur goes over to the printer, taps a button, flicks a switch. "There, that should do it. Want to play, Henry?"

That's Arthur for you: the first message in fifty years is on its way to Omicron and all he can think of is Earth Invaders. He doesn't even look round when the message finally arrives:

"A ship is coming." Arthur's dad's voice has
gone funny. "Here. To Omicron. To this
landing-station. Today." He goes to the
door, flings it open and breathes deep. "We
must prepare, prepare!"

Outside the sun is shining. Beads of water
glisten on the cabbage leaves, the fronds of
the new crop of carrots wave in the breeze.
A vulture is scratching itself in the middle of
a patch of dandelions that have pushed up
through the concrete shuttle landing.

I can see what Arthur's dad means. There
is certainly some preparing to be done.

# 4 – Running Around

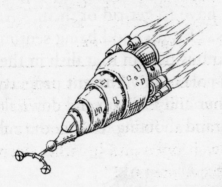

The whole morning I spend running.

I run with Arthur to get his mother to come and help clear up the landing-station. I run to the food plant to borrow things for the manager's office. I run back to the station with my arms full of files and in-trays and envelopes, two telephones and a little rubber stamp saying URGENT. I promise Mum she can have it all back tomorrow when the crisis is over.

Back at the station I run this way and that, cabbage plants under one arm, carrots under the other. Spacemen don't understand gardening. Even if they don't land on the crops, they might trample them. I only stop running in order to dig and transplant. It is hard work. Also there are the vultures. They don't like all the coming and going.

"We'll have to get rid of them," Arthur's mum says. "It's no good being sentimental, they've no business in that dish in the first place. It's galaxy government property."

So Arthur and I run up and down flapping our hands and shouting to scare the vultures.

Then we run up and down flapping our hands and shouting because they are chasing us. We only just make it into the office. As soon as we are inside, the birds float back up to their nest.

"This is ridiculous," says Arthur's dad. "There is work to be done, we haven't even started on the marrows. I bet the manager at Philippon doesn't have this trouble. No, Arthur, that is not the answer. Arthur! I said NO."

Arthur is not listening, he looks like he does in maths. "Honest, Dad," he says, "it will work. What can go wrong?" He fiddles with a dial by the desk and presses a button.

There is a creak and a whine, a flurry of squawking. The dish starts to go round, at first slowly because it's all rusty, then faster and faster.

"Arthur, I will murder you." Arthur's dad lunges for the button, but too late. The whine has turned to a hum, the dish has hit top speed, and there are vultures everywhere, including on the office carpet, and there is a hole in the roof through which they got there. It is lucky going round made them groggy.

While the birds are still shaking their heads and staggering, Arthur's dad throws them out. Then he goes up a ladder and takes the dish down. Arthur's mum and I polish the rust off and then we put it back again the wrong way up. This is my idea, actually.

"I will still murder you, Arthur," his dad says, "but I will put it off till tomorrow. I need you and Henry in the office."

The office is easy. Arthur's mum and dad use the QUEUE ERE sign to patch the roof. Arthur and I spread the files about, open a few envelopes, scrunch up balls of paper and fill the waste-paper basket. We stack up the in-trays and stamp everything URGENT.

"This is what an office ought to look like," says Arthur's dad, rubbing his hands. "One telephone on the desk, Henry, the other by the window. Push the dartboard further underneath the sofa, if I crouch down I can still see it."

"Why should they crouch down and look under the sofa?" asks Arthur's mum. "Do you think they're crazy?"

"They're spacemen," says Arthur's dad.

"They could do anything."

I squeeze the dartboard right underneath the sofa. They will have to lie on the carpet to see it. "Wonderful. If they lie down," says Arthur's dad, "I will cause a diversion. Put the darts under there too, I don't mind where, fit them in somehow." So I stick the darts into the bottom of the sofa.

When Arthur's dad has had his sandwiches at lunchtime, he lies down for a rest as usual. He does not realize the darts are there, not until he has lain down anyway, which shows it was a good hiding-place, in my opinion. He does not see it that way though.

"Goodbye Arthur, goodbye, Henry," Arthur's dad says when he has calmed down. "Shut the door behind you as you go, please. I do not want the birds in here again until tomorrow."

"Are we going?" asks Arthur, and it seems we are. I was getting bored with cleaning up anyway. The ship is not due for over two hours, so there is time for our mock laser fight back at Arthur's apartment. I am bound to win because I have Rolo's pump to use as a laser gun and Arthur only has a bit of metal pipe. Anyway, I am the explorer and Arthur is the alien life form: the explorer always wins.

"Take that, loathsome life form," I cry half an hour later, raising the pump to deliver the death blow. "Perish." I swing the pump down to give him a tap on the shoulder, that's all, nothing violent, and what does he do but swing his pipe up to meet it.

CRACK. Rolo's pump splits into a billion pieces.

"You've broken your pump," Arthur says. Silly twit, as if I didn't know that. "I win."

"It's not my pump. It's Rolo's."

"You're dead, Henry," says Arthur, always ready with a word of comfort. "See you in another life. Want to come in for tea before we go back to the station?"

"I'm not hungry." I am remembering what Rolo said that morning, particularly the bit where he thumped the table and shouted, "You had better believe it, Henry, this time I am not JOKING."

I am thinking that for once Arthur is absolutely right. If Rolo finds out about the pump, my life is over.

It is a terrible thing to have to leave your home and friends (even ones like Arthur and Gonzo) and flee for your life into the unknown. It is even worse if there is no unknown to flee to.

Why wasn't I born on a planet with good ground cover, I ask myself as I enter the apartment cautiously that afternoon. (It is all right, though. Rolo is not in. If he was I would hear him breathing.)

A cave, a forest, a few mountains, I think (putting my ear to his bedroom door to make sure), they would make life so much easier. I do not want much – only a place to hide while Rolo adjusts to life without his pump. A week would be enough. But is there a place like that on Omicron? No, I'm asking you: if there is a hiding-place, I'd like to know about it. I do not want to spend my whole life going through the sort of thing that happened to me this summer.

In case you do not know it, there is only one route out of Omicron, the shuttle to Minimus. The trip takes a week there and back. We did it last year in Environmental Studies. When you come back you say, Well, Omicron is not so bad after all, there are worse places. That's why they make you do the trip.

This afternoon, though, I would stow away on the Minimus shuttle without a second thought, despite the risk of death by boredom. But the shuttle only calls on Tuesdays and this is Wednesday. I can't wait that long.

The clock in the kitchen chimes four times. Rolo may be back at any minute. I must get moving. I may as well go to the landing-station and watch history being made while I'm still in one piece. Then I can say, in the final second before Rolo tears me limb from limb, "Well, at least I saw a ship land on Omicron."

On the way to the front door, an idea hits me. It almost knocks me over, it is such a good one: the ship will land, true, but that is only half of it. After it has landed it will *take off* again. It will zoom up into the sky leaving Omicron, the landing-station, the food plant, the Academy, Arthur, Mr Thomas, Rolo – above all, Rolo – far behind.

I turn back from the front door, my brain racing. I am going to need food, clothes, comics, and something to pack them in. My backpack is torn, so I take Rolo's. He has some clean socks on his bed. I take those as well because mine are dirty. I have read most of his comics but I take a few anyway, in case I get bored, and also his pocket toolkit because it may come in handy. I squeeze everything into the backpack and put some food packets and bars of chocolate on top. I write a note to Mum, so she won't worry.

That's it: my watch says 4.30 and it's time to sprint to the landing-station.

Flight EG 54, the answer to all my troubles, is due to land in half an hour. When it takes off from Omicron, I will be going with it.

I am going to stow away.

# 5 – Arthur's Photographs

Arthur is writing about the spaceship landing for the school newspaper so there's no point my doing it too. It will come out in January, issue 219. You can write and order a copy if you like, when they lift the quarantine. It may be a while though.

In the mean time, here are the photographs Arthur took with his mum's camera at the landing-station. Some are quite interesting.

This was taken at 5.15 when we had been under the desk waiting for the spaceship for twenty minutes. Arthur's dad has just said, "Arthur, if this is a joke I will hold you personally responsible, you will lose ten years' pocket money." I am looking at his leg because there is a spider climbing up it.

When he hears this, Arthur's dad will bump his head and say, "That settles it, I am going home."

The next one is all blurred because of the drizzle on the office window, I told Arthur it would be. You can't actually see the spaceship but that black bit is its shadow. It's lucky we moved the marrows. This one is better because Arthur took it through the open door. It's nice of his dad. That's his best umbrella. He is going to welcome the spacemen.

That's his dad again. He is running now, so it is not

quite straight. You can see the spacemen in the top right-hand corner, but not very well because they are heading in the wrong direction. You can only see their backs. The one at the front has tripped up twice already. They are getting near the hole Arthur and I dug last summer to trap wild animals. "I wonder if they will notice it," Arthur says as he takes the picture.

Arthur was too slow with this one. I know it is hard to get the timing right, but think how nice it would have been to capture the moment when the Captain fell head first into our very own animal trap. Or even the moment before, when the spaceman

with the funny hat tripped and pushed him. Still, you can see here that Arthur's dad is having a hard time getting him out. The hole is three metres deep and full of water. I knew it would make a good trap.

This is one of the best shots. Arthur's dad is talking to the Captain. That black stuff they are covered with is mud. The little spaceman, the Lieutenant, is limping because he's trodden in a gerbil burrow and twisted his ankle. But look at the third spaceman's face – not very pleasant, is it? That is Major Razumov. You can see why I didn't like him.

Now Arthur's dad and the Captain are helping the Lieutenant towards the office.

See that shadow on the ground? The Lieutenant didn't. He is about to feel not very well again.

You can't actually see the vultures here. Major Razumov has stunned one with his hat. Arthur's dad has driven the other two off with his umbrella. The Captain is all bent over because he is dragging Lieutenant Jones towards the office.

This is the last picture on the reel. It's nice of Arthur's parents. Lieutenant Jones has found four of the darts in the sofa. The Captain is soaking wet and covered with mud and there's a big tear on the shoulder of his jacket, but he is smiling. He is about to speak. Do you know what he is going to say? "What a fascinating planet."

I am not joking, I promise. Those are the first words I hear the Captain utter.

I wish the film hadn't run out then, so I could show you Arthur's face, and his parents', and Major Razumov grinding his pointy teeth, and Lieutenant Jones rising up from the sofa as the Captain says it.

"What a fascinating planet."

He is a very nice man and a hero.

*

There are lots of things you may want to know right now. First and foremost, I suppose you are wondering why the spacemen have come to Omicron, why the rest of the settlement are not there to welcome them and wave at the television cameras, how long they are going to stay, and all sorts of things like that. You will know at the right time, OK? Don't rush me.

All right, if you insist I'll tell you why the rest of the settlement weren't there when the spaceship landed.

There were no television cameras because on Omicron we have no television. We have Mike from the *Omicron Press* instead, only he couldn't come because he does martial arts on Wednesday evenings and, as he said, if you miss a class they don't give a refund.

"Try and get them to hang around till 9.30, Henry," he said. "Let their tyres down or something. We're short of news, I could use a story to go after the end-of-term speech at the Academy. It might not be till 10.30, Henry, sometimes I have to have a nap when I'm finished, but I'll do my best,

I promise."

The Mayor and half the council were off in the interior, fishing. The rest of the council were in the interior watching grass grow. This is the major Omicron pastime. I don't think it's any worse than cricket or football.

Most of the teachers and the head of the Academy said they would pop round and watch if they had time, but it was the holidays and they were busy. Mr Thomas was on a ladder painting his apartment. He said, "A spaceship is coming here at five o'clock? Henry, pull the other one. No don't, I didn't mean it, why are you boys so literal, have you never heard of metaphor?" Then he fell off the ladder.

The people at the food plant, including my mum, were also only mildly interested. Professor Robinson, who's in charge, said, "My boy, you see one spaceship, you've seen them all, believe me. I know what I am talking about." I said this was the first spaceship in fifty years to land on Omicron. "So?" said the Professor. "I've heard tell. You find out when you get older, Henry, the only surprises left in life are the nasty ones.

Give my best to the spacemen. I've got a job to do, excuse me."

I went up to my mother's office. She said, "Henry, I have been thinking about your maths, why don't you get your textbook out this afternoon for a while, hm? You could ask Rolo to help you. Trigonometry is so simple, Henry, you are a clever boy, I can't understand how Mr Thomas gave you E for it. I think I will go round after work and give it to him straight between the eyes, he is a lousy teacher. Sure, take the files and telephone, who is there to ring up anyway? Where are you going, Henry, I want to explain about algebra. Henry?" But I am half-way to the landing-station.

So who else is there to form an Omicron welcome party? My fellow students at the Academy? Reginald and George and so on? Gonzo? You are not serious: this is the holiday, they are off at the beach trying to get a suntan through the drizzle. I have no time to chase round after them, I have enough to do already.

Anyway, what does it matter if there are no spectators? Remember this: *I* don't fritter

41

away my time wondering this and that and saying "Why?" and "Just one little point I'd like to mention . . ." I could not care less why the spaceship is coming to Omicron. It would be nice to know, maybe, but it doesn't matter. What matters is to get on board when nobody is looking and hide until the ship takes off, leaving Omicron and Rolo far, far behind.

When I am safe, that will be the time to start wondering, and I am not safe yet by a long chalk.

I still have to stow away.

# 6 – My Plan and Some Minor Problems

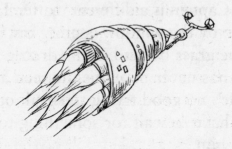

Like all good plans, mine is a simple one.
Mr Thomas says the more complicated the
plan, the more there is to go wrong. Mr
Thomas says it, but I think it is true anyway.
So I am planning to wait until nobody is
looking and then sprint up the steps on to
the spaceship. I don't think you could get
simpler than that: more exciting, maybe, but
not simpler.

Of course, even with a simple plan you can
get problems. Problem one is the Captain.

The Major has taken a book from his
jacket pocket and is busy studying it. Every
so often he nods and underlines something
with a stilo. He doesn't look as if he would
notice me unless I grew wings and fluttered

out of the window. The same goes for the Lieutenant, who is maybe dying, I don't know, his eyes are shut and he is whimpering softly. But the Captain is a different matter. He is standing by the window, staring out at the strip, the grass beyond it, the drizzle falling, as if he has never in all his life seen anything like it. It's no good trying to sneak on board yet. I'll have to wait for something to distract him.

It will have to be something special too. He does not look round even when Major Razumov asks Arthur's dad if there is anywhere on Omicron where he can buy a sub-machine gun.

"Ha, ha." Arthur's dad laughs politely but you can tell he does not like Major Razumov or the way the Major keeps calling him "peasant".

"Ha, ha," replies Major Razumov, but it does not sound as if he means it. He strolls across to the sofa, stamping on Lieutenant Jones' foot as he passes. He sits down hard, lets out a hiss like a kettle, bounces up again, dropping the book. There is a dart in the seat of his trousers. He says something I haven't heard before.

"Major!" says the Captain sternly. "All planets have their customs. We must respect them, however strange they seem to us." He still doesn't take his eyes off the landing-strip.

I pick the book up in case it is worth looking at, but it is only *A Hundred Ways to Get Away with Murder* – probably full of boring jokes like the ones Rolo is always memorizing. It is funny how those books never seem to put people in a good temper.

The Major has taken out the dart and is testing the point on his finger. He weighs it in his hand and makes little stabbing motions. The Lieutenant squeaks in alarm.

"Major!" says the Captain, still without turning.

The Major tucks the dart into his pocket. When I offer him the book, he snatches it without even a thank you. Soon he is back at work with the stilo.

Arthur's dad, like me, has been wondering what on earth the Captain is looking at. He gets up and peers over the Captain's shoulder. But there's nothing out there but the Omicron landscape – or, in other words, nothing. He sits down again, still puzzled.

"You have perhaps a shop that sells small nuclear devices, peasant?" says Major Razumov, stilo at the ready.

Arthur's dad has stopped thinking the Major is joking, he thinks he is crazy. He has no nuclear device, no pistol, no hand grenade, no laser gun, no ground-to-air missile. Would a cup of coffee do instead?

The Major spits on to the office carpet. "Peasant," he says, not in a friendly sort of way. I am beginning to think that problem two is definitely Major Razumov.

And if that's not enough, problem three is the telephones, which are not connected and therefore do not work. Arthur's dad does not mind this, but the Captain has landed on Omicron to restock with powdered food (I told you you would know soon enough). He is on a super-urgent, top-secret mission, and he has to take off without delay. The future of the universe is probably at stake. After an hour or so of playing with the telephone, Arthur's dad thinks it would be a good idea to get the order to the food plant before it closes.

47

"Henry," he says, "would you run over and give your mother this order, please? Arthur, you go too and help carry back the supplies. There's rather a lot. See if you can borrow the Professor's bicycle. Be as quick as you can." It's not the future of the universe that's bothering him, it's Major Razumov. He's never met anyone before who spits on carpets. Say what you like about Omicron, this isn't one of our customs.

"Run along, both of you," says Arthur's dad.

"But, Dad, we were going to play Earth Invaders . . ."

Major Razumov looks up, eyes narrow and nasty like the Head's when there's talking in assembly. "Run, peasants, or I'll drill you full of holes with my laser gun."

Personally, I don't find that sort of humour very funny. Arthur gives me a poke with his elbow. "Come on, Henry."

When it comes down to it, what choice have I? Until they get their food supplies they won't take off again. If they don't take off, taking me along with them, I will have to go home and face the wrath of the gorilla.

Very slowly, I start running.

The next two hours are mostly too boring to
mention. Who wants to hear about stuffing
sixty-nine thousand micro-sachets of powdered
food into packs and hauling them across
country? The food isn't even interesting. It is
porridge, green powdered porridge. This is
not bad stuff in some ways. If you mix it
with water, you can use it to make models. I
would never eat it though.

"Well, someone's going to have to eat it,"
my mother says, as she wheels the bike up
the bumpy track towards the station. "If
they share the food equally, they'll have
twenty-three thousand helpings each. At
three helpings a day, how many years will it
take to finish it?"

I can't work out problems like that. It's
not the maths, it's the thought of all that
green porridge. Ugh.

"A billion years," says Arthur. "Maybe a
trillion. Myself, I'd rather starve. It could
last for ever." It would: all Arthur eats is
peanut butter and jam sandwiches. It has to
be raspberry jam too. He would never make

49

a spaceman.

"I'd be all right on short trips," he says. "I could take a picnic." We argue a bit about whether or not there's any call for day-trip spacemen. Arthur is always arguing.

After a while my mother says that being a spaceman is a silly life anyway. Why travel all that way and then find yourself back where you started? Or, even worse, never get back where you started, but litter up the atmosphere for ever? She says there's no place in the universe worth visiting if it means eating that much porridge. She is right, of course.

I have an idea. "Maybe they're not going to eat it at all. Maybe they're going to do something else with it. Make models or something. Bombs, maybe."

But my mother is fed up with thinking about porridge and even more fed up with hauling it. It's not as if the Professor will pay her extra, she's only doing it to help us.

"I tell you what, I'll take tomorrow off, Henry," she says. "We can go to the beach if you like, it is pretty in the drizzle. Only *please* do not spend the whole time annoying your brother. Fifteen is a difficult age, you will find this out yourself one day."

Tomorrow? I feel terrible.

I have left a note for her on the kitchen table telling her not to worry, but that makes no difference. She will worry anyway. Worse still, she will have no one but Rolo to look after till I get back. She will feel useless. He already knows about algebra and trigonometry. All he ever says is, "I only have odd socks, Mum, where have the rest gone to?" and he only says that on Sunday evening when it's too late to put a wash through. He doesn't understand about her. I have a lump in my throat.

"Tell me how to do quadratic equations, Mum," I say. All the way back to the landing-station, she tells me.

It is so easy to make her happy.

## 7 – Dinosaurs and Spaceships

By the time we reach the office, I have done some thinking. With Mum there, it won't be practical to sneak out of the office and dash up the steps. She would run after me saying, "Henry, where are you going, what is $x^2 + 8x + 16$? Haven't you been listening to me?" and this would put me off. My new plan is very practical. I will have to lead up to it though. People are so suspicious.

"Mum," I say as we dump the bags and bike outside the office, "how would it be if . . .?"

"What's happened in here?" she says, opening the door. "Is everyone dead? Don't say we've brought the food for nothing."

This is a joke. Arthur's mum must have

gone home. His dad and the Lieutenant are draped about the office sleeping. The Major is still making notes in his book and the Captain is still at the window. "Ha, ha," I say, to show I appreciate the humour. "Mum, I was wondering if . . ."

But there's no hope of leading up to anything with Arthur around. "Hey, we can play Earth Invaders now, Henry," he says, before I can finish.

I know Gonzo is supposed to be the stupidest of my friends, but Arthur makes me wonder. Practically all he does is interrupt people and break their pumps and be a thorough nuisance.

I say no, I do not want to play, and after I've said it twenty times, Arthur takes the hint and goes off to play on his own.

Meanwhile, Mum is hunting through her pockets. I give her a nudge but it doesn't work. "Just a moment, Henry. Someone has to sign the receipt for the supplies. Is he in charge?" She means the Captain. "What's he looking at out there? Of course he's looking at something, Henry, don't be silly."

NO ONE ever listens to me. It is enough

to make me glad I am leaving, only at this rate I never will.

She tiptoes over behind the Captain. She looks right, then left. Nothing. Perhaps it's something on the ground? No. Up in the sky then? But there's nothing there either. She shakes her head.

"Sign here, please," she says to the Captain crisply, in case he's deaf as well as everything else. I think it's a long time since anyone spoke so crisply to him from just behind his left ear. It even wakes up Arthur's dad on the other side of the room. "Excuse me," says my mother, "did I startle you? Someone has to sign for the supplies. It's the regulation."

While the Captain signs I have another try: "Mum . . ." That's as far as I get.

"I was hoping," says the Captain as he hands the form back to my mother, "to see an animal before I leave. Do you have animals here?"

Mum says we have animals. "Are you looking for anything special?"

"Not particularly. Aardvark, auk, armadillo," the Captain waves a hand, "they all have their attractions. If I had to choose a favourite, I think it would be the dinosaur – the big one with sharp teeth that looks like Razumov. Do you have dinosaurs like this on Omicron?"

Mum is a quick thinker but not this quick. She says nothing and so does Arthur's dad. A moment ago he thought he had woken up but now he is not so sure.

"Well, it is not important," says the Captain, courteously breaking the silence. "I have the picture in my book to look at. Not to mention Razumov. It really doesn't matter in the slightest. And we must see to the supplies."

My chance at last: "I'll load the food for you. It would be great to look inside a real spaceship." Always give a reason when you volunteer.

"I'm afraid it's a little untidy," the Captain says. "On a long trip there's too much time to tidy up."

"Don't you mean too little time?" Mum asks.

"Maybe," says the Captain. He has a nice smile, but sad.

I say I don't mind untidiness. "And if I

load up, you can go on watching for dinosaurs." The Captain looks wistfully towards the window and I feel a bit mean, but I have to get on board somehow. And if I don't help load up, who will? Lieutenant Jones, whimpering on the sofa as rabbits chase him in his dreams? Razumov, making notes on his cuff from a section called "Simple but effective modifications to garbage crunchers and electric kettles"? I don't think so. Neither does the Captain. He thanks me and says where to put the food.

On my way out, I suddenly realize that this is goodbye. "Bye, Mum. Bye, Arthur." Mum turns, half-way to the window, and smiles, surprised. Arthur grunts from his seat at the keyboard. "See you later then." Arthur's dad gives a gentle snore.

I don't know why I feel so bad about leaving them. They'll probably never notice I've gone.

It takes seven trips to load the food on to the ship. The storeroom is right by the door but there is nothing to stop me exploring much further. The first thing to strike me is that the Captain was putting it mildly: the ship is not a little untidy, it is probably the untidiest place in the entire galaxy.

Look, you know how it is in your own room. Every so often your mum or dad comes in and says, "Right, this place is an absolute pigsty, clear up before dinner or you can't ride your bike this afternoon. How many times have I told you NOT to eat oranges in bed? See this glass, are you looking? This is what happens to old Ribena, not a pretty sight, eh? And this one? How did that sock get in there? No it will NOT wash out, put it in the bin, no wonder you are short of socks." And so on for hours and hours. It is very tiresome, especially when you have just taken a model to bits and are wondering how it goes back together, but in the long run they are right. When you have picked all the stuff off the floor and emptied the waste-paper basket and changed your sheets and cleaned off the windowsill, including that black stuff that comes down from the crack round the window-frame and is nothing to do with you at all, then, I think you will agree, your room is a better and nicer place – for an hour or two anyway.

What you don't perhaps realize is that THIS DOES NOT HAPPEN IN A SPACESHIP. The astronauts do not bring their parents with them. No one makes them tidy up. And their voyage may last for years, for decades, even. You can imagine the result.

The bathroom, for example, is in a shocking state. Is it too much to ask people to put the top back on the toothpaste, for heaven's sake? The fact is, I am going to have to use that toothpaste myself, because I haven't brought any with me, and I don't want the bit on the end that's like cement, do I? Towels all over the place too, I will never find a dry one. No consideration at all for others.

As for the galley (what the rest of us call the kitchen), it's just as bad. Empty food packets everywhere, plastic food trays, paper beakers. If you've got a garbage cruncher, why not *use* it? It is so easy: you put the junk down the chute, you press a button, and thirty seconds later out come lots of neat little bricks, and you can make model houses and all sorts of things with them.

They could have built a fort or a castle or something by the time they reached Omicron. Instead they have nothing but a messy kitchen. It is the waste that upsets me.

It is certainly not going to be easy to find a place to hide that isn't too revolting and full of old chewing-gum wrappers. The galley and the bathroom are out because there's no place to hide there, or in the control room (where there are sheets of paper everywhere except the waste-paper basket). There's nothing else on that deck, I'll have to go up a level.

This is the cabin deck, much more promising. The Captain's cabin would be a nice place to stay because under his bottom bunk there is a pile of comics and a big book called *Creatures that Ruled the Earth*. The bunks have curtains but even so I suppose it would be too risky. Suppose I chose the bunk the Captain uses, I don't see how I could escape detection. The other two cabins are nasty. I bet the sheets have not been changed for twenty years. I could not survive without breathing apparatus. Up to the top deck then. But the rooms there are

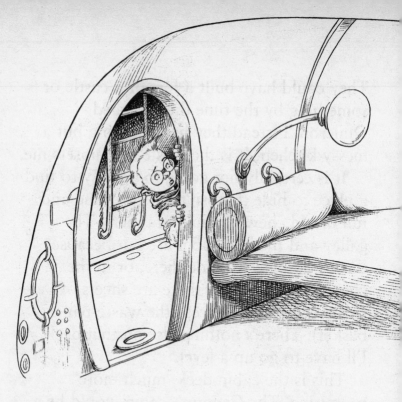

locked except for one the size of a broom cupboard. I couldn't spend even a week inside that.

By the time I have made six trips I am ready to give up. Then I spot a flight of stairs leading down from the entrance, ending at a door marked PASSENGER ACCOMMODATION. Inside it is not too bad. The cabins are about two metres square, the couches are hard and dusty, the washing facilities date from the Stone Age –

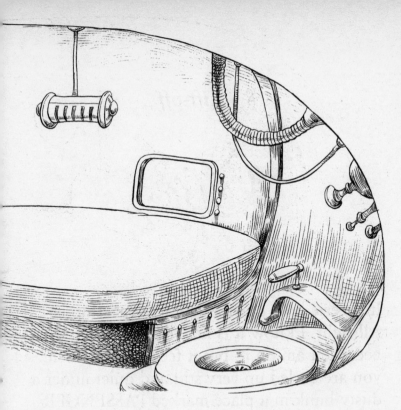

but you can tell by the dust that the crew never come down there at all. It's the perfect hiding-place.

I push my backpack under a couch in one of the cabins and hurry back to the entrance. One more load of food and I can stow away in comfort, more or less, and look forward to a couple of weeks without Rolo. What could be nicer?

People always think things like that on the eve of disaster. It's human nature.

# 8 – Lift-off

It is eerie how quiet an empty spaceship is.
All right, I know it is not really empty
because I am on it, but it feels empty when
you are curled up very still and quiet under a
dusty bunk in a place marked PASSENGER
ACCOMMODATION where no one has set
foot, probably, for fifty years. It is just the
sort of place that might be haunted.

I remember that I hadn't time to check
out all the other cabins. Suppose that in one
of the other cabins there is a skeleton
stretched out on the bunk? It is the skeleton
of the passenger everybody forgot. Suppose
the skeleton ever so gradually begins to stir.
Suppose it sits up on the bunk and puts its
head on one side, listening. I sit very still and

hold my breath, but I can't hold it for ever. In the end I will have to breathe and then it will hear me. Then what?

Then it will pull itself to its feet. It will reach out a hand for the cabin door. It will come out into the lounge, leaving a trail of footprints like a bird's in the dust on the carpet. I won't be able to hear it coming but it will come anyway. It will push open the door of my cabin. It will see my knees poking out from under the bunk, because however hard I try to pull them in, there isn't room enough. It will smile a ghastly smile, worse than Major Razumov's, its jaw will move, it is going to say something terrible, it will say—

"Action stations, everyone. Lift-off in ten minutes."

That's a relief. I was expecting something like: "Henry Hobbs, your hour has come, prepare to meet your doom." I am so relieved it takes me several seconds to realize that someone has actually just spoken those words. The Captain? It must be. But how can I hear him?

"What would happen to us if a rocket

booster exploded at lift-off?"

This is a trembly voice I have never heard before and it sounds as if it is coming from the bunk above my head, which is impossible. It's a good question though. I hadn't thought of it before. What *would* happen if a rocket booster exploded?

"Oh, we would be blown to smithereens," says the Captain chattily. He sounds as if he is sitting on my pillowcase. "We would be utterly annihilated, it would be as if we had never been born, more or less, we would be in a billion trillion tiny pieces. It is strange to think of, is it not, Jones?" THUD. "Jones? Help him to his cabin, Major, he has had one of his turns. I will activate the gravity simulator and start the countdown."

I can hear footsteps receding, along with a heavy bumping noise like somebody dragging a body. A thump and then some rustling, soft, as if whoever it is had paused to consult a book. "Ha!" someone says, then there's a slithering noise punctuated by footsteps growing fainter. Silence.

I wriggle out from under the bunk and stick my head up: I am all alone, thank goodness. What I was hearing must have come through the open tube I can see up by the ceiling. Either that or the walls are like paper. Anyway, I don't feel lonely any more. It is good to know that there are other people near.

"Help," says a trembly voice through the tube. "I'm stuck. Somebody help me."

Lieutenant Jones again, making a fuss as usual. Probably he has a knot in his shoelace and wants someone to undo it for him. I don't think they should let someone be a spaceman if he can't do his own shoelaces.

What's this? THUD THUD THUD, the sound of running feet. A cry of alarm: "Major, give me a hand." It is the Captain. "Jones has fallen down the garbage cruncher – how on earth did he manage that? No, he is all right, thank God. The fuse has blown, remember?"

The Major says the same as he did when he sat on the dart in the sofa.

"Major, this is no time for reading. I *know* he could still suffocate, that is why we must get him out. There, that's better. Don't say anything, Lieutenant, I understand. It was an accident, it could have happened to any of us. Go and lie down for a day or two until you recover. Off you go. Lift-off was one minute twenty-one seconds ago exactly, in case anyone's interested. So the rocket booster didn't explode after all, Jones. You didn't really think it would, did you?"

There is the sound of trembly laughter.

THUD THUD THUD, the footsteps grow fainter. I thump the bunk, I am ready to lie down myself, I have had enough surprises to last a week. But there is one surprise left in store for me.

THUMP THUMP THUMP. A cloud of dust rises from the bunk, thick and brown and full of things unfriendly to the human nose. I huff and I puff and I bury my head in my sleeve, but in the end I can't help it: I have to sneeze.

ATISHOOO!

The sound fills the whole room. It is lucky I remembered to shut all the doors on the passenger deck or they would have heard it, for certain.

"Bless you," says the Captain's voice cheerfully. "Have a good rest, Jones. See you tomorrow."

Night on a spaceship is peculiar. I know there are other people on board because I can hear them. Every creak, scratch and rustle comes through the tube, but I can't tell who is making them or where they are, most of the time anyway.

One or two sounds are easy. The running water must be from the bathroom. Yes: BRUSH BRUSH GURGLE SPIT. Somebody is cleaning his teeth. I am not going to bother with mine tonight, one night off won't harm me. I hope he puts the top back on the tube so it isn't like cement tomorrow.

AAH AAAH. That is the person in the bathroom again. I know what he is doing: looking at his tonsils and wondering why there are so many of them and why one side is bigger than the other. Spacemen are not so different from us after all, are they?

Now what? SCRATCH SCRATCH. Is it the person in the bathroom combing his hair, maybe, or does it come from somewhere else? How does the RUSTLE RUSTLE that I can also hear fit in? I suppose it could be the Major doing his reading. But what about that clanking noise? CLANK SCRATCH RUSTLE. It is like listening to three different stories at once.

Suddenly there is a frightful CLANG CLANG CLATTER CLANK. All the other noises stop dead. It is so still I don't think anyone is breathing even. I'm certainly not.

It seems to me that perhaps an engine has fallen off or someone has forgotten to shut the spaceship door. I wish anyone was there, even Rolo, to tell me what is happening.

"Is that you, Lieutenant? Are you all right?" That's the Captain's voice.

There's a pause and then a shaky "I'm asleep." What a terrible liar – even Gonzo could do better.

"Major?" asks the Captain.

SNORE SNORT SNORE. Not very convincing. So the Major is a liar too. That doesn't surprise me.

I bet it was him who made the noise though. Because now I have started breathing again, I know what it was. It was somebody using a chisel. Well, it could have been a screwdriver, but a chisel is my guess and I have dropped enough tools to tell the difference. What was he up to chiselling away in the middle of the night, with nowhere to go but deepest space? That's what I'd like to know if I were the Captain.

It's none of my business though. I would sleep if I could, but the ship is so noisy.

"One . . . two . . . three . . . four, five, six,

seven . . . eight, nine . . . ten." Someone else can't sleep either.

"Eleven dinosaurs, twelve, thirteen, fourteen . . ." The counting goes on and on until I begin to feel sleepy. "Forty-six, forty-seven . . . forty-eight, forty-nine . . ." WHUMP, someone punches his pillow. "Where was I? How many dinosaurs is it? Oh no, I will have to start again." WHUMP GROAN WHUMP.

"Fifty," I say softly, "you'd got to fifty." Silence.

"I didn't know anyone was still awake," says the Captain. "Thank you, Jones. Or is it Razumov?"

I don't say anything.

"Fifty dinosaurs, fifty-one, fifty-two . . ." I don't know how many dinosaurs there are altogether because suddenly I am fast asleep.

## 9 – A Million Miles from Home

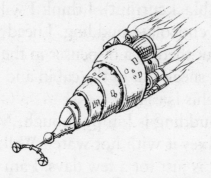

When I wake up again the porthole above the bunk is black. I spit on a corner of the bunk cover and rub the glass, but it makes no difference, except to the cover – the glass is still black. I almost decide to go back to sleep but then I realize: there is no sun in deepest space, no light. There are no clouds, no wind, no falling rain. There is no weather. It is exciting, and something else, I'm not sure what. I have never been so far from home.

When I have finished cleaning the glass, I'm hungry. Time for breakfast.

No cornflakes and vegetable substitute here, and I ate all my chocolate last night. I'll have to eat one of the packs I brought with me. There's chocolate pudding, cheese and potato pie and dried gooseberry yogurt (I can't think how I came to bring that, I only eat blackcurrant). I think I will start with the chocolate pudding. I need water to mix it, but there is a dispenser in the passenger lounge. I sneak out of the cabin and fill a beaker. This is easy.

The pudding is lumpy though. Maybe Mum mixes it with hot water. Well, it doesn't matter, it is just for a few days. I am not a twit like Arthur who would die without his peanut butter sandwiches. A few lumps don't bother me. Actually, I am not that hungry.

The beaker is half full of brown sludge. I put it under the bunk until I can throw it away.

Now what? My watch says 8.30. Surely the rest of them ought to be up by now? I can't hear a sound though. Are they all still asleep? Who is driving the ship then?

Perhaps they are not asleep. Perhaps a mystery virus has wiped out all the crew, like in one of Gonzo's books, and I will have to fly the ship myself all the way back to Omicron. This will be exciting: I do not know how to fly a spaceship and I do not know the way. That is the sort of thing you ought to learn in school really, not geography and paragraphs and maths.

BRRRRRRR, a bell rings right by my ear. I almost jump out of my skin, wondering whether this means "Fire!" or, "Abandon ship! and where is my parachute?" Then CLICK, the bell stops. "Time to get up, men," the Captain says.

I should think it *is* time. Fancy not setting your alarm until almost nine o'clock on a super-urgent, top-secret, extra-galactic mission. I don't think Mission Control would be very pleased if they knew *that*, or that the crew spends all morning doing absolutely nothing. They hardly talk even. It is very boring for a stowaway. In class I can at least write notes to Arthur. Here it is difficult to do anything. I'm not complaining, but honestly it is difficult.

To give you an example, I can hear somebody humming – humming so badly it would be a public service to help him. So I join in, quite softly.

HUMhumHUMMMM, he says. Painful to listen to.

HUMMMhum HUHUMM, I say. You would have to be deaf not to hear that this is better. But when I've only hummed it three times he starts screaming: "Stop it, stop it. I know what you're doing, you're trying to drive me mad, well you won't succeed, you have been stealing my socks too, why have I never got a matching pair, I know what you're up to now so stop it, just stop it." THUMP THUMP.

THUMP THUMP? I'd rather not know what that was. Suppose it was him hitting the other two on the head with a blunt instrument: would you want to know that you were on a spaceship being driven at a million miles a minute into nothingness by a very touchy murderer with odd socks? I didn't think so.

Anyway, it wasn't that. Nobody has been hit on the head, because I can hear the Captain telling Razumov that Jones is under the weather. That's bound to happen to spacemen from time to time. It happens quite a lot of the time actually.

Soon I am under the weather myself. I have counted the tiles on the ceiling, the squares on the floor, the panels on the walls. I have made a tent with the bunk cover and tried to imagine I am camping, and in a few minutes Gonzo and Arthur will come in with a bag of chocolate cookies and we will eat them singing songs round the campfire.

It is no good, though, without the cookies and Arthur and Gonzo. Especially the cookies. I am so hungry I could eat anything. Even the stuff in my backpack? I'll try. Maybe this time the chocolate pudding will not have lumps.

It does. Soon there are two beakers of sludge under the bunk. Then I have my brainwave: If I add a little more powder the sludge will be perfect for model-making.

I will give myself something to do and solve my rubbish problem.

To make the mixture thick enough, I have to add all the packs of gooseberry yogurt flakes and four of cheese and potato pie. Then it is brilliant, although a funny colour, a sort of swampy green. There is enough for four snakes, a couple of small lizards and a dinosaur with spikes. I like the dinosaur best. It has a happy expression. It has just come out of the swamp and seen a friend.

I will call it Arthur, to remind me.

CLANG CLATTER CLANK, the chisel hits the deck again, just in time. I was getting homesick.

"What's that?" asks the Captain sharply. In deepest space, these noises get on your nerves. It's such a long way down.

No one answers. Either they're deaf or somebody is up to something. I don't think they are deaf.

Later on, when everyone else is asleep, I will take a good look round. If somebody is up to something, I don't want to be the last to know. Besides, there is the top-secret, super-urgent mission to think of. The fate of the universe may be in my hands, mine, all disgusting and caked with green sludge that is very difficult to wipe off and has made a bit of a mess on the bunk cover. I can't wait for night, so I can clean them with hot water.

For supper I try the cheese and potato pie: yellow slush with lumps in. Under the bunk it goes. I will ask Mum what I am doing wrong when I get home.

Home. Omicron. Every moment it is further away.

I'll never be a spaceman, ever.

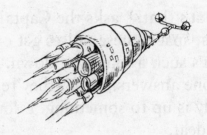

Of course, tonight of all nights the Captain has to stay up late. At 10.30 he is still on the prowl.

PAD PAD PAD KNOCK. "Hello, Jones, you would not care for a game of chess, I suppose. Oh no, another time maybe. We have lots of time after all, there is no shortage of *that*, is there? How is your work progressing these days? Oh, please don't do that, Jones, we all have moments of depression. Here, take my handkerchief. And cheer up, you will feel better tomorrow. I will say good-night, then. Good-night, Jones."

PAD PAD PAD along the corridor to the Major's cabin. KNOCK. "Hello, Major, you have been cleaning your guns again, I see.

And your knives too. What is this little spiky thing for? On second thoughts, I would rather you did not tell me. Is this the book you are always reading, may I have a look at . . . No, of course, if you would rather not . . . There is no need to sit on it, Major, I was merely asking. Well, I will check the doors and windows before turning in. Good-night."

WHUMP, a door shuts. SIGH. That's the Captain. He is fed up with Jones and Razumov, anyone would be. It is hours before he sleeps, and what seems like hours more before I can be sure nobody is going to get up again. I can't afford to get it wrong and bump into someone in the bathroom. I don't even have a dressing-gown.

I think that first night when I finally creep up out of the passenger accommodation is the nicest night of my life. The water in the bath is hot and bubbly, there are ducks and a wooden boat to play with. All day I have been shut in a tiny cabin, sneezing from dust and feeling, I don't mind telling you, pretty miserable. I have never enjoyed a bath so much.

Everything else is wonderful too, like magic.

I stroll through the control room towards the huge screen by the control panel. A tiny blip is flashing near the top right-hand corner. The label underneath says "Flight EG 54". It's us – I am on that blip, the only one awake for a million miles probably. I am in the Captain's chair piloting an extra-galactic space cruiser on a top-secret mission. What is this button here? Shall I press it and send us rocketing backwards? What about the ON/OFF switch at the side? Shall I switch off and see if spaceships float? I'm not really going to press anything, but it is fun pretending.

As I get up from the chair, my hair catches on something. There's a spike stuck in the upholstery just above where my head was. It's not any old spike either: it's the dart Major Razumov took from Arthur's dad's office, only it's been sharpened and someone has torn the flights off. If I'd been a bit taller, I could have had a nasty accident. I hate that sort of carelessness.

There is another chair in front of the control panel. I can't be sure who it belongs to, but if there are two chairs and three people, something tells me Major Razumov

isn't going to be left standing. So I push the dart up through the seat of the second chair carefully, so you would have to look very hard to spot it. That will teach him to mind where he sticks his dart in future.

Now I feel even better than before because I have done something useful. What else could I do to help? The room is a mess like everywhere else: someone has sat on the log-book so that it is coming apart, and sheets of printer paper are everywhere. That's easy to put right. I tidy the loose leaves back into the log-book and then I pick up the printer paper and stuff it into my back pocket. I can use it to make paper darts tomorrow.

I empty the ashtrays into the bin in the galley, and while I'm in there I fix the fuse in the garbage cruncher with Rolo's toolkit. That will be a nice surprise for the Captain tomorrow – nicer than the one he almost had anyway. I don't know who had been tinkering with the wiring, but he obviously didn't know much about garbage crunchers. I mean, the switch wasn't so much a switch as a detonator. Press it and next thing you would be a billion tiny garbage bricks shaped like spaghetti. It's lucky for someone I'm here to put things right.

Time for a last visit to the bathroom. I clean my teeth *and* put the top back on the toothpaste. I hang up the towels and let the water run out of the bath. I can't do anything about the bubbles. I expect they'll be gone by morning.

Morning? It *is* morning. The happy night is over and I have to get back to my cabin. I haven't found out what the chiseller is up to either. Never mind, I think as I shut the door to the passenger deck behind me. There's always tomorrow. And the next night, and the night after that.

Do they come, those other happy nights? Yes and no. They come, but they are not so extra specially happy.

Unknown to anyone, most of all me, I have just stuffed into my back pocket along with the printer paper several sheets from the log-book, sheets containing information of a vital and shocking nature. I am about to discover the TRUTH about the secret mission of Flight EG 54.

*

Yes, at last we have got there: the secret of Flight EG 54. It has been a long time, hasn't it? Even longer for me than you. You don't have to mess about looking up words and putting in paragraphs to please Mr Thomas. I don't know why I bother.

It is not as if you are going to be surprised really. You may not realize it, but you already know what Flight EG 54 was up to. You saw the headlines, you yawned through it on television while you were waiting for the cartoons, you may even have seen *me* if you didn't choose that moment to get a Coke from the refrigerator. Yes, you know it all – except for the bits that matter.

For a start, you do not know what it is like to find out from the back of a paper dart that you are on a flight that is due to last fifty years. Think about it. If you are ten, like me, when you find out, you will be ready for your pension by the time you see home again. Fifty years. Mum will be a little old lady. Rolo will be a grandfather. Arthur will have given up Earth Invaders.

Wait a minute, you might say to yourself: I am not going to stay that long. I'm a stowaway, not a spaceman. When they find me, they'll turn back to Omicron and I'll be home in a week. Yes, you might say that, but not for long. You would soon start to read the other papers you stuffed into your pocket the night before, in that other life when you were happy, and find out that on a super-urgent mission the ship does not turn back for *anything*. It goes on and on until its mission is accomplished. Then and only then does it turn round and zoom back to the nearest landing-station.

Well, you might think then, maybe its mission *will* be accomplished. Things are not so bad after all. What *is* its mission, you ask yourself, and then you find out and wish you hadn't. For the mission is no less than this: to explore the furthest limits of the known universe in search of new forms of intelligent life. Not just "life", please notice – "intelligent life". Something like Arthur or Gonzo will not do.

There is a message from Mission Control explaining this in detail and a lot of long words. It ends:

Roll back the frontiers of human knowledge, Captain. Boldly go where no others have trod before, and return with unimaginable treasure in your hands. You MUST succeed. You WILL. Goodbye, Captain. Good luck.

PS If you don't succeed, don't bother coming back. We can't afford another failure.

The date at the top of the message is 27 January 2153. Yes, 2153. They have been on their super-urgent mission *nine* years already and they have only reached Omicron. I don't think they are going to accomplish anything in a hurry. There's more too:

PPS Sorry to hear about Engineer Schulz and Navigator Barnard. I am sure Electrician Razumov was in no way to blame: wiring on electric kettles can be a tricky business. Since it is impossible to supply replacement crew or kettles, can only suggest you promote Razumov again and use a saucepan in future.
Best wishes, Mission Control.

This is a terrible moment. I am heading for deepest space on a hopeless mission along with the worst electrician in history. It is not a good situation.

Forget what you think you know right now, please. Forget the headlines and the newsreels, and later on the hourly bulletins, the grave faces, the President of the Galaxy, the soldiers with laser guns and all the rest of it. This is the TRUE story, the one you will never hear from anyone but me.

Flight EG 54 is searching for new forms of intelligent life. I am searching for the way home.

I MUST succeed. I WILL.

# 11 – A Near Thing

What a person with a problem needs is a little peace and quiet to solve it. You would think that on a ship heading for deepest space I could find that, wouldn't you? Wrong. It is about as peaceful as Mr Thomas' maths class. Yesterday they were so quiet it was boring. Today I can't hear myself think.

If I could, I think it would be easy. Because of course things are not so bad as I thought. There are hundreds of ways I could get home. They need thinking through, that's all.

For instance, I could use Rolo's toolkit to do something to the engine. They would never be able to repair it themselves, people who can't even change a fuse. We would have to go back to Omicron. I would be home in no time.

Where is the engine though? We must have one, or we wouldn't stay up. I'll have to find it and then I'll have to make it go wrong. Not too wrong, that's the tricky thing. It's trickier than I thought, especially when the interruptions start. It is like a madhouse, one thing after another.

I mean, first of all Major Razumov is on at the Captain to go and try out the garbage cruncher because he's got it working again. Anyone can tell the Captain doesn't want to because he is in the middle of a game of chess with the ship's computer, but at last he says yes, he will go and try the cruncher.

"Aren't you coming too, Razumov?" he asks, just as I'm trying to decide if it would be better to snip a wire or loosen a bolt. "Why are you wearing that crash helmet? Are you expecting us to crash?"

I do not care what the Major is expecting, I have more important things to think about. Maybe instead of fiddling with the ship's engine, I ought to turn the ship round secretly in the night. The only thing that shows which way we're going is the blip on the control screen. If that started going backwards, would anyone notice? I shouldn't think they look at the screen mostly.

"Yes, it does work," says the Captain's voice. "Well done, Razumov. Are you looking for something under that table, Major? Why don't you come out then? That's better."

But it isn't, not for me anyway. Now it's the Lieutenant's turn.

"What is that, Captain? What is that up there on the screen near our ship?" Trust Jones to have nothing to do but stare at blips and get excited. There is nothing near the ship, I bet. It is a bit of dust probably.

"Mmm," the Captain says, very calm. "It looks familiar but I can't quite place it. This is most interesting."

"What is it, what is it?" It sounds as if he is screaming right in my ear.

"I don't know what it is, Lieutenant. A meteor maybe."

"A meteor? What will happen if it hits us, Captain?"

That's not such a bad question. What *does* happen to a spaceship if it collides with a blip that is maybe a meteor?

"Oh, the ship would be wiped out," says the Captain. "We would be as dust drifting in the infinite spaces between the stars, that sort of thing. I did not know you were interested in philosophy, Lieutenant."

THUD.

"Ah, now I remember, it is not a meteor, it is the cue for my game of chess. Nothing to worry about, Lieutenant. Lieutenant?" Then there is more fuss, sploshing water, the sound of a body being dragged away. More like maths class every minute.

I think my best chance of getting home fast is to get the printer to print out a message along the lines of:

```
Go home immediately. Ask no questions.
Important message awaits you on Omicron.
Yours sincerely, Mission Control.
PS Ask no questions.
```

If only I knew how to work the printer this would be a truly brilliant idea, taking into account the meteor and the garbage cruncher, and the fuss and commotion when Major

Razumov sits down by the control panel and finds his own dart. I'm glad it was him who found it, he could not be more dangerous if he was *trying* to kill someone, but honestly – even when they all stump back to their cabins not speaking to each other, I can hear Jones sobbing and the Major kicking the spaceship walls. It is too much.

"SHUT UP," I shout, "I'm trying to THINK."

There is an awful silence. I didn't mean to say it. It just slipped out.

"I was not doing anything," says the Captain, rather chilly. "There is no need to get upset, Jones. Or is it Razumov?"

Silence.

"Well, we must all make allowances, I suppose. We will say no more about it."

Whew. That was a near thing. No more thinking for me until they are all asleep.

# 12 – Trapped!

At 11.30 that night I creep out to the bathroom, stopping only to pick up more modelling porridge from the stores. It is all right mixed with cold water but I think it may be stickier with hot, and if I mix up a basinful to get stodgy while I have my bath, I can make some friends for Arthur before I start serious planning.

It is better with hot water. Soon the basin is brimming with green stodge. I squirt plenty of bubble mixture into the bath and jump in. It is a good feeling blowing bubbles and chasing the ducks with the boat while no one in the whole universe knows what I am doing or where I am. It is especially good compared with what happens next.

BBRRRRRRRR WHEEEEEWHHEEEEE
BBRRRRRRR WHEEEEEEEEEEE!

What on earth . . . ?

"Everyone to the control room immediately,"
says the Captain's voice briskly. "Action
stations. We have an emergency."

An emergency? What sort of emergency?
Is it the sort where you get in line and file
out in silence (do not panic, boys, the bomb
will not go off for twenty seconds)? How
will I be able to do that, all wet and covered
with bubbles? I had better get out of the
bath at once – but no, I have left it too late:
they are all in the control room together, the
Major snarling, the Lieutenant bleating. If I
make a move they will hear me and goodbye
all chance of seeing Omicron again until I
am old and grey like Mr Thomas.

"There is no need to panic," says the
Captain (I wasn't *really* panicking), "but
there is an intruder on board the ship. I have
had my suspicions for some time and now I
am certain. You know what this means,
Lieutenant? Major? Yes, our mission is
nearing its end. We will soon be face to face
with the new form of life that has eluded

mankind so long. An alien has boarded us mid-flight – metamorphosed, probably, aliens are always doing that. We will search the ship for it room by room. Steel yourselves for what you must expect to see." I am panicking after all.

"What must we expect?" asks a trembly voice. Yes, what?

"Oh, a loathsome form of life, repulsive, slimy, that sort of thing," says the Captain, very chatty, "possessed of sinister powers we can only guess at, out to destroy us mind and body into the bargain, I wouldn't be at all surprised. I personally think it will have green tentacles and smell like decomposing socks, well, we all have our own theories and we will soon find out."

I do not like the sound of this. If I had known there was a slimy green alien with tentacles on board I would never have come. And last night I was wandering about all over – I could have bumped into it a dozen times! I hope they find it soon because I am definitely not leaving the bathroom until they do.

"We will start at the top of the ship and

work our way down," the Captain says, "although I think I know where the loathsome creature is lurking. I have heard it, Major, swishing its deadly tentacles and making alien bubbling sounds that would make your blood run cold. Yes, Lieutenant, I have little doubt that we will find the alien in the bathroom."

The bathroom? THE BATHROOM? The alien is in here with ME? Surely not! I would have noticed even a very small green thing with tentacles. Unless it were invisible? If I listen very hard, maybe I will hear it.

But all I can hear is the PAD PAD PAD of feet elsewhere on the ship and the soft POP POP of bubbles and my own breathing.

Then the truth dawns. The alien IS in the bathroom with me. I AM THE ALIEN. The Captain has been listening to ME.

"No, the alien is not in your cabin, Jones," says the Captain. "And I am not surprised either, it is high time you changed your sheets. Your cabin next, Major."

They are searching the ship. At this rate they'll reach the bathroom in – what? Ten minutes? Even if I could sneak back to the passenger deck without being caught, it wouldn't be any good: they will go on searching until sooner or later they find me.

This is a desperate situation, and I can see only one way out.

With a little imagination and a lot of green porridge, I can save my skin and give Flight EG 54 the best of all reasons for heading home.

I, Henry Hobbs, am about to become an ALIEN.

There is no time to lose.

I jump out of the bath. In seconds I have dried myself as much as possible on the soggy towels and dived into my clothes. Why shouldn't a new life form wear trousers and a sweatshirt if it wants to? Besides, I will run out of porridge if I try to cover my whole body. There's only enough for my head, hands and feet.

PAD PAD PAD, the hunters are on the move. Where are they now? GASP COUGH SPLUTTER CHOKE – entering the murk of Razumov's cabin, by the sound of it. I had better get moving.

I roll up my sleeves and take a last look

at the face in the mirror. Goodbye, Henry Hobbs. I plunge my hands into the basin of green stodge and scoop up as much as I can.

SPLODGE.

The world goes dark. When I open my eyes again, my face is a green blob. Hello, alien.

There is no time for anything fancy like tentacles or antennae. SPLODGE SPLODGE on goes the porridge anyhow, over my hair, into my ears, down my neck. The face itself is difficult because the porridge cracks every time I move my mouth, but I add big splotches here and there so this won't show so much. I porridge round my glasses until only the two lenses are left showing. I can't leave them off or I won't be able to see.

Now for the feet and ankles. I sit on the bath and put my feet in the basin. STAMP KICK SPLOSH. In no time I have a pair of green splodgy feet. The hands come last of all – once I've done them I won't be able to do much else. They will crack too, each time I move my fingers, but that can't be helped. If they are nice and knobbly no one will notice.

PAD PAD PAD SLAM, they have finished with the Captain's cabin. Time is running out. On with the taps to sluice the remains of the porridge out of the basin. I mustn't leave the evidence behind.

Is there anything I've forgotten? Too bad. It is too late to do anything else, too late for second thoughts, too late to wonder how aliens behave and what they say to strangers. The door is opening, ever so slowly and cautiously, but opening. I can hear the Captain whispering, "Have the laser gun ready, Razumov, but remember, we want the alien ALIVE."

"Grawk." I think this is the sort of thing an alien would say when it is relieved. Three faces are peering round the door at me. "Grawk!" I say again and smile to show I am a friendly alien. Crack goes the porridge.

"Aaargh, there it is, revolting, inhuman, look at its eyes, like some terrible insect, and its skin all green and cracked like the living dead, horrible, horrible, I cannot bear it AAARRRGGGH." THUMP, the Lieutenant folds on to the floor. I didn't think I looked *that* bad.

"Greetings," says the Captain, stepping neatly over the body. "Greetings, small green alien humanoid. He cannot understand me, of course, Major, but he may sense that we are friendly and not do anything sudden."

"Look as if you're so much as thinking of doing anything sudden, disgusting green alien," says the Major, "and I'll zap you from here to Philippon. Do we understand each other alien? I hope for your sake we do."

"Grawk." I understand the Major only too well and I am certainly not about to do anything, except try to keep breathing. I wish I felt as sure about the Major.

"Major, we will handle this my way, please. We are friends, little humanoid. We have come to invite you to our homes, we want to get to know you. Would you like to return with us to one of our planets?"

"Grawk." Every time I smile, the porridge cracks all over.

"It's not interested," says the Major. "I can tell. I'd better shoot it." He lifts the gun.

"GRAWK GRAWK!"

"No, Major! You're wrong. It's put its hands up, I mean its paws up. Stop waving that gun about, for heaven's sake. You're frightening it. Put it DOWN, Major. That is an order."

"I'm watching you, alien. Move a paw and you're dead. Try it, alien. Make my day." He lowers the gun maybe ten centimetres.

"Grawk," I say pleadingly. The Major is worse than Rolo, *and* he has a laser gun, which Rolo doesn't. I think I made a mistake stowing away. Maybe this is the moment to say, in a casual way, with a laugh, "Ha, fooled you. I'm not an alien at all. I stowed away on Omicron." No one shoots stowaways. Or do they? Because before I say anything but Grawk, I'd like to be sure.

"Uncanny, isn't it, the way he seems to understand? What we have here, Major, is a very intelligent life form," the Captain says, "which shows you cannot go by appearance. Put the gun DOWN, Major, I will not tell you again. That's better. Now, you revive Jones while I escort the alien here to the control room and turn the ship around. I will take the gun, thank you, just in case. Kicking will not do Jones any good, Major, have you forgotten your first-aid course?

Come this way, humanoid. I will see that nobody harms you. We are going to be friends."

My plan has worked! He is going to turn the ship round and head for home! I had better stay an alien after all.

## 13 – How to be a Good Alien

This is the beginning of a strange period in my life. I have never been an alien before, except in games with Arthur, and there the alien always ends up dead. I can see now this is not fair. Aliens have a right to live, like anything else. Their ways are not our ways, as the Captain keeps telling Lieutenant Jones, but that is not their fault, is it? We are none of us perfect, especially Major Razumov who is always creeping up behind me saying "ZAP ZAP, alien, you're dead", which anyone can see is not the way to make an alien feel wanted. If I ever bump into a real alien, in that dark corner of the garage where no one has set foot for a hundred years or maybe underneath Rolo's bed when

I am looking for his rugby boots, I will never ever behave like that.

Being an alien is not easy. It is no good just crouching in a corner pretending to be dead so the Major will not shoot me. If I am a very boring alien, maybe they will decide to look for something better instead of going back to Omicron. So I do my best to be interesting. I flap my arms a lot and say grook grook sometimes instead of grawk, and when I go anywhere I walk backwards. This is difficult to remember and I keep bumping into things but if you are going to be an alien, you may as well do it properly.

Well, this is lost on Major Razumov. He could not care less how interesting I am. It is because of me that he is going to go down in history as the discoverer of a new life form, but he is not even grateful – he acts as if he would rather go down as the man who wiped me out. Whenever the Captain turns his back, there is Razumov with his laser gun, snarling, "All right, humanoid, why don't you try something? Are you feeling lucky?"

"Grook grawk." This is what aliens say when they are miserable, but they say it very softly in case they get shot.

Lieutenant Jones is not much better. He stares at me and says things like, "My god, my god, it is horrible, look at its flippers, have you ever seen anything so revolting?"

They are not revolting and they are not flippers. They are paws, as anyone with a little sense can see. I waggle them to show him. SPLODGE, a lump of porridge falls on to the carpet.

"AAARRGGHH, it is disintegrating before our very eyes," he cries, the silly twit. That sort of language is offensive to an alien, but I cannot bother about him now. I have to decide what to do about the bit that fell off. It won't stick on again and I can't just leave it on the carpet. Well, it is only porridge, after all. I may as well eat it, goodness knows I am starving and no one has thought to offer me any food. It doesn't taste bad actually.

"AAARGGHHH, it is eating itself, oh, the horror, the horror." THUD, he hits the floor again. He is too excitable to be a good spaceman.

One thing an alien thinks a lot about is

food. You wouldn't think I'd have to point this out, would you? Everything needs to eat. The trouble is, I can't be too obvious about it. I can't say, "When's lunch?" or help myself from the storeroom. I have to ask for food in an alien way. So when I see the plastic food bowls coming out, I wag my head and say "Glub glub."

"Look at it, Major," says the Captain, "what a fascinating humanoid it is. Perhaps it is feeling ill or perhaps it has an itch between its shoulders that it cannot reach, we can only speculate. Pass the porridge, please, Major. It is like opening a door into another world, is it not?"

"Glub GLUB." If I wag my head any more the whole lot will fall off. Who cares about being fascinating? I want to be fed. I try reaching out, to get the point across.

"Lay a flipper on my bowl, alien, and you're history. Go on, try it."

I don't want to be history. I reach out cautiously and point at Lieutenant Jones's bowl instead. A small knob, a very small knob, falls off my hand into his porridge.

"AAARRGGH, disgusting, loathsome,

107

revolting, I am poisoned, I cannot breathe, I am suffocating." THUD.

This is very embarrassing. On the other hand, while they are hauling Jones back to his cabin I have the chance to nip down to the bathroom. Aliens need to do this too, you know, and if I am quick I can be back in the kitchen before the Captain and the Major return.

"It only *looks* as if it wants to eat our food, Major," says the Captain, coming back into the room. "Its energy system will be far beyond our comprehension – magnetic forces, negative ions, it could be anything. What mysteries will be unravelled when the scientific team that is being shipped to Omicron get a chance to observe it closely."

It is no good expecting an alien to be interested in a team of scientists when it's hungry. It is like asking Gonzo to think about algebra ten minutes before lunch. Speaking of lunch, on the table is Lieutenant Jones's half-eaten bowl of porridge. Very carefully I sneak towards it (it is hard to sneak backwards, no wonder there are so few of us aliens around). There is more than half a bowlful! Slowly I stretch out a paw and pick up the bowl, slowly I lift it towards my mouth—

"ZAP ZAP, alien, you're dead."

Slowly I lower the bowl, untasted. If the Major doesn't get me, starvation will. Will I ever see Omicron again?

## 14 – Only a Story

In the days that follow, time ceases to exist, just as in science workshop, but unlike in science workshop I learn some strange and interesting things. I am going to tell you them, whether you want me to or not. That is like science workshop too.

First of all, I learn about the Captain. I am sticking to him like glue to make it harder for the Major to shoot me. When the Captain goes to the control room, I go. When he patrols the ship, I follow him. When he retires to his cabin for a rest after lunch, I am right behind him.

"I will see you later, alien," he says, nipping inside and shutting the cabin door quickly.

"Grawk! GRAWK! GRAAAAWWWWWK!"

"Well, you can come in if you like," he says, opening the door again, "if you are quiet and do not disintegrate on the carpet."

He sits down on the bottom bunk and fishes out a comic from beneath it. I like comics. I take one too.

"You are holding it upside down, alien," the Captain says after a minute. "Look, hold it like this."

"Grawk." Having cunningly established that I would not know a comic from a hole in the atmosphere, I can safely climb up to the top bunk and enjoy a quiet afternoon's read. Or so I think.

"It is nice to have company, alien, make yourself at home," says the Captain, popping his head up and giving me a serious shock. "No, do not eat the comic, it will give you stomach-ache, besides I have only read it 1,495 times already. That is better. I do not mind if you use it as a hat. There, I will make one too."

The Captain puts his comic on his head and we look at each other. My nose is itchy. I scratch it, through the porridge. The Captain scratches his nose too.

"What are you thinking of, I wonder, alien?" the Captain says. "Do you have what we would call a mind? I like to think so. Do you have a mother, a father, brothers, sisters, friends? Do you have a home, alien, are they wondering where you have got to, have they put your dinner in the microwave to keep warm? You are snuffling, alien, I wonder what that means."

Never mind snuffling – all this talk of home is making me feel terrible. I must be brave, however, because aliens do not cry – also because if I cry my face will melt. "Grawk," I say softly between snuffles, "grook." I wipe my nose on my sleeve, and then on the Captain's handkerchief, which goes green and sludgy. Well, it could have been worse. I could have lost my whole nose.

"It is as if you understood me," the Captain says, tossing the handkerchief into the waste-chute with deadly accuracy, "which is, of course, impossible. To you, I am the alien, that is a funny thought. Well, I hope I am not as alien as Razumov. I do not think I could be. Do not be sad, alien, if you are sad. Take the comic off your head, if that is your head, and we will look at it together."

"Grawk." Anything rather than talk about mothers and brothers and friends. And, of course, dinner.

So we look at the comic. It is a Western, with a good cowboy in a white hat, called a sheriff, and bad cowboys in black hats. There are Indians and gun-fights and bank robberies, and at the end the sheriff says, "Reach for the sky", and the ones with black hats put their hands up. It is a good story. The Captain explains it all, right up to the end.

"Now the bad men go to jail and everyone is happy. The sheriff waves and rides off into the sunset. Do they have horses where you come from, do they have sheriffs, do they have sunsets? Do they have stories? You cannot understand a word I am saying, can you? Never mind, it was only a story. Only a story, but why can't life be more like the stories, alien? Maybe it will be one day. There will be good people and bad people and we will always know which is which and the good people will always win. That would be a future worth waiting for. Do you think it could be like that some day, alien?

I think it could."

"Grawk!" I say doubtfully. "Grawk?" I never know what to say to those questions. Of course it would be nice if the world was like that, but nobody wears hats on Omicron. As a matter of fact, we don't have horses either. The sheriff could ride a gerbil into the sunset, I suppose, if he could find one big enough and if it hadn't settled into rain as it does around half-past four most afternoons. It might work. Maybe.

The Captain is pointing at the last picture again. "Look," he says, "this is grass, alien. There is grass where we are going. Grass and dinosaurs and flying animals called birds and people who do not carry laser guns. It is a very nice planet. I had forgotten what a planet was like until I landed there. Twelve years in middle space, alien, nine on inter-stellar exploration, three years as apprentice on the lunar shuttle, ten years at the Orbiting Academy, five years in space kindergarten . . . I am forty years old, alien. Forty years and I have never seen a dinosaur. Maybe I will see one this time, maybe we will both see a dinosaur."

114

"Grawk, grawk?"

"No, it is no use looking out of the window, alien. There are no dinosaurs out there. There is nothing out there, nothing at all. The glass is like a mirror, alien. All you can see is your own face."

Something strange happens as I look into the black glass. Suddenly I want more than anything else to lift my hands to my face, peel off the crust and say: Look, I'm no more an alien than you are. I'm Henry, from Omicron. I only want to go home.

I don't know why I want to do this.

And anyway, I can't.

# 15 – Exit the Major

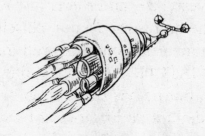

Later that evening, I am in the circular hall on the top deck nibbling my porridge crust where it won't show and thinking that we never know what life has in store for us and maybe it's just as well, when a familiar sound breaks the relative silence.

CLUNK CLANG CLANK.

It is very loud, and it seems to come from the bit of the hall I can't see instead of through the tube – which, now I come to look at it, has been stuffed full of socks. Socks! Of all the surprises I have had in space, I think this is the most puzzling. Are they special socks or would any socks do, I wonder? I am just thinking that I will have to ask Mr Thomas when I get back, and ought I to do it in science or in home crafts when it happens again:

CLANG CLATTER CLANNNNNNKK.

So I investigate, and there, just round the bend of the hall is the Major, chiselling away like anything at a section of wall marked ESCAPE HATCH. Why he is doing this I do not know, but he has the laser gun on the floor beside him and it does not seem wise to interrupt. I have a hunch he may be up to something.

I am right.

"Ah," he says after a terrific CLANG CLUNK CLATTER. "Done it. Now what comes next?" He gets the book out of his pocket. "Murders in space, murders in space, where is it? Here it is. 'File through the hinges'– right, done that. 'Test to see that the escape hatch is now working properly.' Mmm. Who can I test it on? Jones? No, I am saving him for later. The alien, then?"

I would like to scream for help, but my brain has frozen and my lips are numb. My paws are rooted to the spot. I would faint if I wasn't afraid he would hear the thud and come and find me.

"No," says the Major several lifetimes later. "Mission Control are expecting it, it must be spared. Besides, when I am Captain, the glory of discovering the loathsome object will be mine, all mine. So I will have to leave out the testing and go on to the next bit. 'Ask the victim to inspect the escape hatch'" – the Major rubs his hands and chuckles softly – "'and push him through at the earliest opportunity.' Right. So the next move is to call the Captain."

"How is he going to do that?" I wonder, but my paws already know the answer. As the Major's footsteps approach along the corridor, I scamper out of sight ahead of him. Now I'm by the escape hatch looking down at the laser gun the Major has left there, and he's where I was, by the socked-up tube. I can still hear him though.

"No need for these any more." There's a plop as he pulls the socks out. "Captain, Razumov speaking. The escape hatch on level four seems to have jammed. Inspection requested. Over."

"On my way, Major."

At any moment the Major is going to come back round the corner and find me. I'm not ready for this. Without any decision on my part, my paws pick up the gun and scurry through the only door on that level that will open, into a sort of empty cupboard where I can hide until my brain starts functioning again. Which it begins to do almost immediately. I mean, it's all very well to take the Major's gun, but what am I going to do with it? I don't know the first thing about laser guns. Do they have triggers

119

or buttons or what? Can you shoot them inside a spaceship without something awful happening?

ZAAAAAAPP!

You can, and without even meaning to. I haven't the faintest idea how I did it, but by my left foot there is a hole in the carpet the size of a cricket ball.

THUD THUD THUD. This is not me having a heart attack, it is the sound of feet approaching along the hall. The Captain and the Major are coming. And I haven't had time to think of anything yet.

"This is the hatch, Captain."

"I see. And you say it's jammed, Major?"

"Try for yourself. Give it a push with both hands. It's jammed solid."

This is it: if I don't do something fast, the Captain will push the hatch, the hinges will give way and that will be that. No more Captain. I can't let that happen. So I do the only thing I *can* do. I open the door and step out, ready to say: "Reach for the sky." But before I can speak, several things happen at once.

ZZZZAAAAAAAAP. The gun goes off

again, burning a hole in the carpet in front of the Major.

"?***!*?" The Major jumps backwards, landing on the Captain's foot and losing his balance. He grabs at the wall to steady himself but it isn't the wall, it's the escape hatch.

WHUUUMMMMMMPPF. The hatch opens and closes so fast I think I must have dreamt it, but when I look at the place where the Major was, there is nothing there.

"AAARGH," says Lieutenant Jones, choosing this moment to appear in the hall and getting the wrong end of the stick as usual. "Have pity, alien. Mercy, mercy, do not shoot, I will be your slave for ever. I will do anything only do not shoot me—"

I turn round to give him a reassuring grawk and ZZZZAAAAP it happens again without my doing *anything*, there must be something wrong with the gun.

"Have mercy, great being, mighty ruler of the universe, I grovel before you, I hide my face from the brilliance of your compound eyes, I am as the dust beneath your enormous green flippers. I did not like to mention it before but I worship you, alien—"

121

ZZZZAAAAAP THUD. Honestly, it is
not my fault and there was no need to faint,
it didn't even touch him. Some people get all
worked up about nothing. I think he had
gone mad anyway.

"Er . . . alien, if you pass me the gun I
will show you something interesting, it is
called a safety catch," says the Captain
sitting up (he has been lying on the floor for
some reason, with his hands over his head).
"Here it is. Now I am going to press it.
There. Now there will be no more accidents."

I can't believe it but I am still in one piece.
And the Major is gone, which is a good
thing. And I haven't shot anybody. And I
haven't let on that I am not an alien.
Everything is going to be all right! Any
minute the Captain will get up and haul
Jones away, and then, who knows, I may at
last get to eat a proper dinner.

The Captain is not in a hurry to move
though. You would think he had had a
shock or something. Ah, now he is stirring.
He's beginning to kneel up, one hand on the
escape hatch to push himself off.

On the escape hatch?

122

"Don't!" I yell, launching myself through the air and catching the Captain round the knees with the rugby tackle that has brought me planet-wide fame as second reserve on the Omicron Academy C squad. "Don't lean on the hatch! The Major cut the hinges, I saw him. You'll fall out too!"

The Captain freezes, everything freezes. There is a terrible silence, terrible. Slowly he takes his hand off the hatch.

"Grook!" I say, all at once remembering who I am. I let go of the Captain's knees and pick myself up, shedding bits of paw everywhere. "Grawk!" But I know it is too late.

Henry the alien is finished.

## 16 – My Last Evening on Board

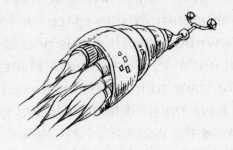

It is not as easy as you might think to tell somebody that you are not an alien. It is a bit like telling them you have broken their space buggy pump. I mean, you know they are not going to be pleased about it. However, when a thing has to be done, it has to be done.

It is a relief that the Captain takes it so well, even the bit about stowing away, which of course has to come out too, or how would I be on the ship in the first place. Also the bit about Major Razumov trying to murder him, and the dart and the garbage cruncher and Schulz and Barnard from long ago. I hope it will cheer the Captain up, because he is looking very thoughtful. He hardly smiles though. Something's bothering him.

"What is it?" I ask when he has been staring thoughtfully into space for five minutes without touching his porridge.

"Oh, nothing, alien. I mean Henry."

I have some more porridge myself, and when I have finished he is *still* doing it.

"What's the matter?" I ask again, because when I was an alien I couldn't help noticing that he was a very quick eater. I never had the chance to pick up any scrapings from him.

"Nothing, Henry." He gets up and leaves the table without having a spoonful, so I know it is something bad. A major mechanical failure? A navigational malfunction? An attack by meteorites, a fuel leak, something too awful to tell me?

"No, Henry," the Captain says, "it is true I am a little preoccupied but there is nothing to worry about. Nothing for *you* to worry about, that is. Excuse me, I must take the Lieutenant his tranquillizer. No, I think it would be better if you did not come with me. I don't want to do any explaining this evening. Tomorrow will be soon enough."

This is my last evening in space and I ought to be feeling happy, what with having washed off the porridge and having someone to talk to at last, but the Captain is not in the mood for talking. He doesn't even want to read comics with me. He stares into space and sighs often, and at last he sits down at the desk in the control room and begins to write. But he is not happy doing this either – he writes a line and then scrunch, he crumples the paper into a ball and throws it on to the carpet. He does the same with a second sheet, and a third.

I can't help if I don't know what the matter is, so I pick up a couple of sheets and smooth them out.

This is the first:

```
FLIGHT EG 54 TO MISSION CONTROL. IT WAS
ALL   A   MISTAKE.   CANCEL   EVERYTHING.
SINCERE APOLOGIES.
SIGNED THE CAPTAIN.
```

This is the second:

```
FLIGHT EG 54 TO MISSION CONTROL.
ALIEN HAS DISAPPEARED SO HAS MAJOR
RAZUMOV. PLEASE CANCEL MEDAL CEREMONY,
SEND SCIENTISTS HOME, NO NEED FOR
INTER-GALAXY TELEVISION COVERAGE.
KINDLY ACCEPT RESIGNATION.
SIGNED THE CAPTAIN.
```

"Resign? Stop being a spaceman? But why?"

"Well, Henry, it's like this." Having gone this far, the Captain comes to a halt in order to frown at another sheet of paper. Then he sighs. Scrunch. "Everyone thinks we've found a new form of intelligent life. They probably thought we'd never do it, but when we did they were very excited. There are television teams setting up their cameras tonight on Omicron, Henry. When we step down off the ship the world will be watching, including the President of the Galaxy and the Director of Mission Control. At this very minute a team of nine scientists is flying in to study your unique biological system. When all these people find out that there's been a mistake, they will be disappointed. They will be more than disappointed, Henry, they will be annoyed."

I hadn't thought of that. "Annoyed with *you*?"

"Who else is there?" The Captain picks up a new sheet of paper. "Besides, it is my fault. I should have guessed you weren't an alien, Henry. I wanted to believe you were one too much. I didn't want to spend the next thirty years with Jones and Razumov. You were better to talk to, Henry, even when all you said was grawk. That should have told me. I should have known."

"Anyone can make a mistake."

"Not that mistake, Henry. That is a special sort of mistake, the sort that makes you famous from one end of the galaxy to the other. Wherever there are televisions and newspapers, people will hear the story of Flight EG 54. And when they hear it, you know what they will do, Henry? They'll laugh. At the Space Programme, at the Director of Mission Control, at the Galaxy Government, and, above all, at me. There is the Captain, they will say, who couldn't tell a boy from a humanoid. I do not think they will promote me, Henry. You don't get promoted for making jokes."

"What will they do to you?"

"Oh, arrest, court martial, loss of pension rights, imprisonment, disgrace. Something along those lines. It is not that I blame you, Henry. It is going to be a little awkward, that's all."

The Captain smiles and puts down his pen. "Well, this will do as well as anything. I had better send it and get it over with."

```
FLIGHT EG 54 TO MISSION CONTROL. THERE
IS    NO    ALIEN.    REGRET    ANY
MISUNDERSTANDING. SUGGEST YOU CANCEL
RECEPTION. FULL REPORT AND RESIGNATION
FOLLOW. SIGNED THE CAPTAIN.
```

"I wish I'd never *been* an alien!"

"That wouldn't help," he says, sitting down at the keyboard.

"I wish I *was* an alien after all!"

"That would, but it would be a little difficult to arrange, I think. Where is the letter C, Henry? It is always where I can't find it. Henry? What is the matter?"

The matter is that I have had an idea, an idea the like of which I have never had before, because never in the history of the whole galaxy has there been an idea like it.

"It wouldn't be at all difficult to arrange," I cry. "We have plenty of porridge, don't we?"

"I do not see, Henry . . ."

"And we have a whole day to mix it up and put it on before we arrive on Omicron!"

"Put it on what? I still can't find the C, Henry."

"On me, of course! I *can* still be your alien. I can be green and crusty, I can have feelers and tentacles and big pointed ears this time, I've always wanted to try those. I can wave at the cameras and say grawk to the scientists, and when you have got your medal and nobody is looking, I can nip off

131

out of sight, wash it all off and disappear!"

"It's a nice thought, Henry," says the Captain, "but it would never work. I shall miss you when I am in prison, you know. Perhaps you could write to me every couple of years if you are not too busy. You could tell me about Omicron, send a picture of a dinosaur, that would give me something to look forward to."

"You're not *going* to prison. It *would* work. It WILL! It will be easy, you'll see."

"It will NOT be easy, Henry, and it will NOT work."

"You're wrong," I shout. "I'll show you!"

Looking back, I can see that he was not so wrong as I thought he was going to be. You could even say that he was very nearly right.

# 17 – The Homecoming

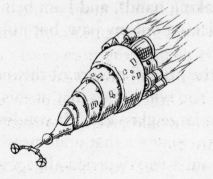

Well, I have written a lot more than four pages and the rest of the story is history. Like me, nearly. A picture is meant to be worth a thousand words, so here are some pictures. (I don't think Arthur's are worth a thousand, though. Four words is more like it.)

Here is the first picture Arthur took of me coming down the steps with the Captain. It's not too bad considering who took it. I am waving at the cameras. The people in uniform at the foot of the steps are the Omicron Academy orchestra. Half of them are getting ready to play the Omicron anthem on their recorders, the other half are getting ready to play "Hail the Conquering Hero". The Omicron anthem won, but only just.

Here is a proper picture by Mike from the *Omicron Gazette*. The Captain and Arthur's dad are shaking hands, and I am behind the Captain sticking out my paw, but nobody will shake it.

This is the official picture of the medal ceremony. You will notice that at this point I am inside a large glass cage. If you look carefully you may see that underneath all the porridge I am a very worried alien, because things are not going as I imagined, and although the glass cage has little holes at the top to breathe through, it is going to be hard to disappear from. The Captain is looking

worried for the same reason. Arthur's dad is looking at my feet because the porridge is crumbling off and he has noticed that the new life form is wearing blue trainers like Arthur's.

This is one of Arthur's pictures again, you can tell, can't you? I know he was excited but it only takes a second to get the camera straight. Who on earth is going to want a picture of somebody's right shoulder? I don't want a picture of this man at all actually. It is the chief scientist having an argument with the Captain and Arthur's dad after everyone else has gone home. He wants to load my

cage on to a special laboratory space cruiser and take me to pieces to find out how I work. Arthur's dad is looking noble, he has just said: "This alien is an honorary citizen of Omicron, I demand you let him go", but the chief scientist won't.

This is another of Arthur's pictures. At least he has got the Captain in properly this time. What the Captain is pointing at is me in the cage, although of course Arthur has left that out as usual. The Captain is saying something along the lines of: "Good heavens, just look at the alien!" I am lying on the floor of the cage grawking feebly, the very picture of an alien on its last flippers. It would have been a brilliant photograph but that is Arthur for you.

Look, you can just about see my head down at the bottom on the right of this shot. You can also see the Captain's chest, Arthur's dad's arm and a flap of the scientist's overall. Another triumph for Arthur. The Captain is saying: "I warn you, the alien will disintegrate at any moment if it is not taken indoors at once and allowed to rest. How will *that* go down at Space Headquarters, well, you must be the judge of that, it is your career after all, you are a brave man to take the risk." The scientist is not saying anything. He is thinking though.

At last, a decent photograph of me. Even Arthur could not get it wrong from as close as this. The cage is in the hut now and I am looking over Arthur's shoulder to where the Captain is mouthing, "Do not worry, alien, it will be all right." I know he will do his best but maybe that will not be good enough, so I am not looking happy. One of my antennae has fallen off.

There are no pictures of me at night. You will have to imagine me sitting in my cage as far away as possible from the scientist with the big gun who is guarding me. It's not the way I thought I would spend my first night home, I can tell you.

Morning again, bringing the Captain and Arthur's dad, and of course Arthur and camera, keen to snap a few photographs of me being dissected, I expect, to sell to the school magazine. This is me waking up and wondering what is going on and catching sight of my tentacles before I remember they are only porridge. When I come round, the Captain is saying: "Great galaxies, it is as I feared. Pray God that we are not TOO LATE."

"Too late for what?" asks the scientist with the gun. Yes, what?

"I cannot bear to say it," the Captain says, "it is too terrible to think of. Let me examine the alien at once, the future of the galaxy may depend on it—"

"AAAAAAAHGGHHHH!" shouts Arthur's dad from the other end of the room, nearly giving me forty fits. "What is that?"

This picture is not Arthur's fault really. It is dark down that end of the hut and it is a trick anyway. All I can say is, I wish someone had told me first, that's all. In a minute the Captain and the scientist are going to go rushing down there, and they will find – a horrible pool of green sludge such as nobody likes to see first thing in the morning. On my planet pools like this occur naturally when someone drops a plastic bag of green porridge which he has been keeping up the front of his jacket. You get them all the time at school (I expect Arthur showed his dad how to do it) but the scientist is not to know that.

"What is it, what is it? Eeugh!" he says. "It looks just like the alien but how could it be, he was in the cage all night. I must get the chief scientist, help."

Off he goes at a gallop.

And now they will let me out, I think, but no, the Captain dives into the cage with me. How will that help? I want to ask, but I have temporarily forgotten how to speak. "Grawk!" I say pleadingly instead.

"It's no good letting you out, Henry," he

says. "They will be back any minute. What we are going to do is better, we are going to get rid of the alien *and* the scientists for ever, permanently, once and for all. It is going to work, I promise."

It had better work too, my proboscis is falling apart.

"Grawk?" I ask, but feet are pounding on the path outside, and the Captain is crouched in a corner of the cage with his back towards me. He is doing something to his face, I think, but I can't see what because he is hunched over.

The door bursts open and the scientists rush in. "Get out of that cage at once," shouts the chief scientist. "This is an emergency! Everyone leave the building."

The Captain stands up slowly and turns round. "It is too late," he says quietly, shielding his face with his hands. "Too late for me, too late for us all, I fear. The worst has happened. Run for your lives! Warn the townspeople! The alien has PODDED!"

Then he lowers his hands.

"AAAARRRRGGHHH! His ears, his face, his skin, he is turning into an ALIEN!"

The room is empty.

I'm glad Arthur got that last photograph right. He is not a bad alien, the Captain, is he?

# 18 – Back to School

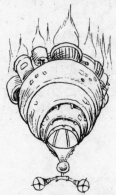

Basically, that is what I did in the holidays. I know there was another week after I got back, but that was when they had the state of emergency, with armed squads of Galaxy Government soldiers combing the planet for escaped aliens. Mum hardly let me go out even. You don't want to hear about that.

The soldiers searched our apartment like everywhere else, but the closest they got to an alien was meeting Rolo. I had gone back to being Henry, and the Captain was being Mum's Cousin Alfred on a visit from Minimus. Nobody recognized us at all.

The soldiers have gone now, and the scientists. They found someone else to fly the spaceship wherever it was going, but they left Lieutenant Jones behind in case he was turning into an alien too, on the inside where nobody could spot it. I think it's for the best: he's not cut out to be a spaceman.

When the soldiers left, the Captain went to help Arthur's dad at the landing-station. Arthur's dad says he has never seen anyone so good with potatoes. After lunch they take turns on the sofa.

"I broke your pump, Rolo," I told Rolo when I got home that morning. "I'm very sorry."

"What pump?" says Rolo. "Oh, that one. It doesn't matter, it hasn't worked for years. My *real* pump is in the drawer with my vests. Just let me know if you ever want to borrow that one, or you will be in *real* trouble. Are you all right, Henry? What's the matter?"

One day, when I have nothing else to do, I'll tell him.

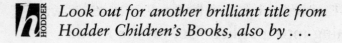

*Look out for another brilliant title from
Hodder Children's Books, also by . . .*

# Kathryn Cave
## Illustrated by Chris Riddell

# William and
# the Wolves

William's little sister Mary has lots of
annoying habits, but the worst is her
invention of an imaginary friend. Not just
any old imaginary friend, but a *lamb*.
The rest of William's family think Mary
is adorable, and humour her, but
William is irritated.

Now *he's* invented some imaginary
friends. Only there are six of them.
And they're wolves. It looks like Lamb
could be in for a shock . . .

*Another classic from this award-winning
author and illustrator team.*